# Four Fierce Kittens

## Joyce Dunbar

### Pictures by Jakki Wood

**ORCHARD BOOKS**

*For Joanna*
*J.D.*

*For Rebecca Neal    Molly Martin*
*Alexandra Burkart*
*J.W.*

ORCHARD BOOKS
96 Leonard Street, London EC2A 4RH
Orchard Books Australia
14 Mars Road, Lane Cove, NSW 2066
First published in Great Britain 1991
First paperback publication 1992
Text copyright © Joyce Dunbar 1991
Illustrations copyright © Jakki Wood 1991
The right of Joyce Dunbar to be identified as the author of this
work and of Jakki Wood as the illustrator has been asserted by
them in accordance with the Copyright, Designs and Patents Act, 1988.
A CIP catalogue record for this book is available from the British Library.
1 85213 241 8 (hardback)
1 85213 309 0 (paperback)
Printed in Belgium by Proost

Fat mother cat was asleep on her mat.

Said her four little kittens,
"There's no fun in that!"
And they went off round the farm to run wild.

Said the marmalade kitten,
spiking her claws,
"I am a terrible tiger!
I shall hunt hen out of her hutch."

And she tried to growl
(But she didn't know how)
She could only go...

miaow miaow

And hen went

CLUCK

CLUCK

CLUCK

Said the black little kitten,
with a glint in his eye,
"I am a panther on the prowl.
I shall frighten pig out of his sty."

And he tried to howl
(But he didn't know how)
He could only go...

And pig went

# OINK OINK OINK

Said the tortoiseshell kitten,
pricking his ears,
"I am a leaping leopard!
I shall chase duck into her pond."

And he tried to snarl
(But he didn't know how)
He could only go...

miaow miaow

And duck went
QUACK QUACK QUACK

Said the tabby little kitten, twitching her tail,
"I am a dangerous lion!
I shall make the sheep run down the lane."

And she tried to roar
(But she didn't know how)
She could only go....

And the sheep went
# BAA BAA BAA

Said the four little kittens, ever so fierce,
"We are tigers! Panthers! Leopards! Lions!
We shall scare that gaggle of geese!"

And they tried to roar,
To snarl, to growl,
And they managed to go....

miaowl miaowl

But the geese went HONK

HONK

HONK

Then a puppy came over to play.

Those four fierce kittens arched their backs.
Their fur stood on end. They hissed. They spat!
And that terrified puppy ran away...

Said those proud little kittens,
"We didn't know we could do THAT!"

And they went back to their mother,
to sleep on the mat.